CW00996178

CHANG

A novelette by Lesley Atherton
First published by
Scott Martin Productions, 2018
www.scottmartinproductions.com

First published in Great Britain in 2018 by
Scott Martin Productions
10 Chester Place,
Adlington, Chorley, PR6 9RP
scottmartinproductions@gmail.com
www.scottmartinproductions.com

Electronic and print on demand versions available for purchase on
Amazon.

Many thanks to Morrigan Atherton-Forshaw for the cover art.

how will we tell dominic?

'How will I tell Dominic?' she cried. 'How *can* I?'

I wanted to answer with something definitive, wise and non-negotiable, but I just couldn't. I'd known her all my life - she was my sister, my best friend and my inspiration. And we both knew that, no matter how carefully Maggie or anyone else told Dom, he'd not necessarily understand, and even if he did, he'd immediately be sucked into a grief of unimaginable intensity.

Because, for him, it was only the two of them who really mattered - Maggie and Dom: Mum and son alone in a world of near-strangers: a claustrophobic but beneficial symbiosis where only their duality had meaning.

'I suppose I *do* have to tell him?' Maggie's eyes were puffy and streaming with silver tears, her head cocked onto one side like an accident-prone puppy begging for forgiveness: begging for help.

'Somebody needs to,' I said.

I knew that.

And I knew it would be me.

what will dominic do?

Maggie had always buried her head when it came to Dominic. Her ferocity came to the fore when negotiating face to face with tangled bureaucracy for the protection of her boy, but when it came down to the difficult stuff - anything that might upset Dom, or anything that required long term planning, responsibility or form filling - she struggled, and that was when I stepped in. Good old reliable Auntie Sal.

Maggie's day-to-day existence with Dom didn't follow the lines I would have chosen had Dom been my child. In fact, Maggie's approach would have left me in perpetual panic. I'm the responsible one; the organised one; and the one who deals in details - while Maggie deals with Dom. It's the very nature of his condition that's made it that way. He's a long term commitment, even more so than most children, as Dom was never destined to leave home after three years at college. He's Dominic: with all that being Dominic entails.

It always worried me that Maggie never came to terms with addressing the universal fears of single parents everywhere. She hadn't written a will or taken out life insurance or private medical care. She has always lived on a wing and a prayer. Sometimes life with her is like flailing unprotected on the wings of a primitive aircraft, and sometimes the prayer is more desperate plea than calm supplication.

At least Dom is more realistic – if that's the right word. An example. About six months ago, when Maggie started getting symptoms and was waiting for her first consultant's appointment, she asked him (in one of our usual and almost daily tests) what he would do if she wasn't able to care for him.

'I will kill myself,' he'd said, without thought or consideration. Not 'would' but 'will'. No theoretical musing, more a statement of intent. From anyone else it may have sounded melodramatic.

Maggie had looked away from him and began busying herself with the seemingly never-ending stream of washing up.

She inhaled deeply and loudly, with breaths that were clearly audible over the sound of hot running water. Once again, Auntie Sal came to the rescue.

'Interesting,' I'd said, ensuring I did not look up from my coffee cup, for fear of that being interpreted as confrontation. 'That's a shame, love. That would be such a shame. You're only thirty-something.'

'Thirty-three,' he'd corrected. I knew. I'd been there the day he was born, holding little Maggie's hands as his body tore out of hers.

'OK, thirty-three. So, how do you think you would kill yourself, then?'

'I would stop breathing forever,' he'd replied. 'Forever. Actually, not forever. Just till I get to Mum again. I'll meet her in heaven and I'll start breathing.'

'And then what?'

'We'll play chess.'

'And will you let her win?'

'Of course not. That would be cheating. You can't cheat in heaven.'

And then Maggie had laughed her forced little laugh and had reached over to stroke Dom's sleek black hair with her hot, dripping soapy hand. He'd backed off, pulling away from his Mum's single gentle touch with just the hint of a pained grimace.

diagnosis day

Yesterday we sat, staring at grubby waiting room magazines, awaiting Maggie's almost inevitable and damning diagnosis. After flicking distractedly through the magazines, Maggie opened her bag and removed a folder. From the folder, she drew out a watermarked writing pad. Blue paper, crinkled and comforting, it was the same paper we'd both used to write our childhood thank-you letters. She rummaged around for her blue fountain pen and began to write with a slightly neater version of her usual almost unreadable script.

'Using time wisely,' she said.

It is part of the human condition to know there's a clock ticking for each of us. But Maggie's timer was malicious and impatient. She had tears and fears in her eyes too: she turned her head away, but still I saw them.

Maggie being Maggie wouldn't let me acknowledge the existence of the tears and fears that lay behind her words, and I knew better than to ask about them.

But I could see them. I could feel them.

I knew what she was writing too – without needing to read those hastily scrawled letters. Later she claimed it was just a list of questions to ask the consultant, written to keep her thoughts fresh and to help her move on. But I knew she would never have used that watermarked pad for scribbled notes. She'd never have used her special pen either. No, that was saved only for the most crucial of communications: communications to Dom. He was both her greatest pain and her most exquisite pleasure: the problem and its solution.

As children, our spacious four-bedroomed family home had plenty of space for all four of us, yet Maggie and I had insisted on sharing our room, our thoughts, and even our clothes during our entire childhood and adolescence.

Inevitably, that kind of closeness grants knowledge. I could read a single expression of Maggie's and turn it into a compound sentence. I could tell how she was feeling by the way she styled her hair, not just by the words she spoke...

And even then, as we waited for Maggie's consultant appointment, and as we patiently sat for thirty-two minutes past our designated time slot, I knew that she was writing to Dominic and expressing her death sentence, in words and phrases she hoped he would understand.

As soon as we were released from the consultant's room, Maggie returned to the same chair and finally allowed her tears to flow. I crouched in front of her and pushed her white hair behind her ears.

'Don't,' she said. 'I can't cope if you're nice.'

I remained crouching in front of her, my hands cupping the red canvas jeans where they covered her pained knee joints. I kept my hands there, warming some of the pain away. She sighed, loudly and deeply. I was all she had to keep her strong.

'I don't know if I can do this.'

'You can. I'll help.'

'Yeah but you can't go on living your life just for me and Dominic.'

'I can't think of any better people to live my life for.'

We sat in silence for a while as the waiting room filled and emptied, filled and emptied. Again, I suspected what was going on as I've seen her working through projected conversations with Dominic many times and sometimes out loud she'd ask for help in a barely discernible, whispered, desperate plea.

'How should I tell him?' the conversation would begin.

'Darling do you understand?' she'd suggest. 'Your Mum isn't going to always be here, and we have to think about what to do when I'm not.'

Or she'd consider 'Sweetheart, we're all getting older. Everyone dies. You are likely to live for longer than me. It doesn't mean I'm a bad mum, or that I want to leave you. It's just the way of the world of life and death. It's sensible to make plans'.

Or 'Let's have a day out. We could drive to a great place you might like to live in. You'll make so many friends'.

But, however she phrased it, Dom's imagined response would be the same: that blank look he's had since babyhood. It was a look that told of how he understood the individual words and could use them wisely himself. But it was also a look that made it clear that when his mother spoke and strung those words together in her own particular way, they lost all collective meaning in a jumble of senselessness.

I'd planned to stay overnight with Mags and Dom on diagnosis day, but she asked me to leave. She now knew the name of the evil disease that would gradually make her life more and more difficult (till it didn't any more). She needed time to get accustomed to the knowledge.

And we both knew that Mags had to make plans sooner rather than later - for Dominic, if not for herself. Dominic was Maggie's genetic link with a future she's unlikely to experience herself.

She'd already resigned herself to not seeing any grandchildren. Dom was most unlikely to experience his own continuance of the species, get married, have children, or forge any kind of successful career - or even much of an independent life. Sure, he could wash and feed himself and use the bathroom. Mostly he could also dress himself and use the kettle and microwave. But he couldn't cross the street or use the phone. He couldn't talk to authority, or write a letter, or select his meals. He couldn't even be relied upon to get himself out of the bath as he has no feeling for when how much time has passed or when the water's cold. Left up to Dominic, he'd also stay in bed all day, though he's not a lazy young man. It's just that life's transitions are a mystery to him.

about dominic

I couldn't love him more if he'd been my own baby, but Dom's always been an intensely idiosyncratic child.

For him, something must be just right, or it is not at all right.

Black or white.

All or nothing.

Even as an infant, Dom bypassed the usual experimental stage (mama and dada and 'what's that?') and instead threw himself immediately into short discussions with words pre-formed and meanings already clear. I'm not suggesting he was some kind of prodigy or genius as his speech was late to come and we were in and out of hospital diagnostics and speech therapy appointments when he was a pre-schooler. But once those sentences arrived, they flowed fully formed.

He was a clever kid who bloomed into an equally clever adult – you only need to visit his bedroom and read his notebooks to know that - it's like he's on a mission from another planet to log the weather on planet earth.

I remember with fondness how he begged for a chemistry lab to be set up in his room and how Maggie and I both had weeks of sleepless nights over the prospect. Eventually, after taking advice and speaking in much depth to Dom, Maggie agreed. Dom paid for a gas canister and bunsen burner from his spending money, and would order metals and powders and liquid through the post.

There was no real danger. Dom was the type of student who read, who read around the subject again, and then only when he was completely aware of the results of any experiment, would he complete it at home, logging it entirely at every miniscule stage into his set of navy blue, A4-sized spiral-bound notebooks.

second parent

I don't think Mags would contradict if I was to describe myself as Dom's second parent - and I guess I might even be his confidant.

But Maggie was the nurturer, the day to day carer, the one who cleaned wounds, washed laundry and experimented with great frustration to get him eating different foods. Food was the hardest hurdle to cross. At the age of 15 Dom ate his first olive, by mistake of course, and if Mags had owned bunting and fireworks, she might well have celebrated that achievement on the street – doubtless much to the disdain of her teen son.

And I remember the time we persuaded him that he might find cheese and onion crisps even tastier than his strictly-adhered-to ready salted. With Dom's approval, we set up a blind taste test as a science experiment. I bought a blue A4 spiral-bound pad of the type he was already accustomed to using. Maggie was to be the scientist project leader and I was to be the scientist's assistant, accurately recording all results according to the criteria that Dominic had himself set.

Dom demoted his Mum and became self-appointed scientist, with Mags and I as his assistants. This 19 year old experimenter was ready. Ten or fifteen years ago there weren't quite the crisp flavours and varieties that we see now, but there were still plenty to choose from. Once Dom had agreed to the experiment, Maggie and I excitedly visited all the local supermarkets and purchased as many single packs as we could find - from highly spiced corn snacks to the unsalted plain potato chips I'd remembered from my own childhood. I had to also purchase a couple of packs of disposable bowls, otherwise Dom would have preferred only those in the bowl that he knew, or if we hadn't decanted into bowls, he would have liked the sound of some packets better than others, and that would have influenced his opinions of the tastes involved. It wasn't only taste that was to be scored – each crisp was also to be scored for smell and texture from behind a blindfold – then only later to be judged on their appearance.

In the end, Dom's blind crisp tasting had to be abandoned as this picky and careful eater had become carried away, forgetting himself and his usual ritualised behaviour. His mouth was so full of ten different types of crisps that he was unable to score anything on their individual crunchiness, freshness, spiciness or anything else. The experiment's outcome was simply that crisps are great. And since then he's eaten every type he's offered, apart from roast chicken, which he says tastes only of stuffing, and that the name, and therefore the packaging are blatant lies: I know this because he tells me every time we enter the supermarket's crisp aisle.

Of course, it wasn't surprising that Dom found his taste test fun, so Mags and I capitalised on that and used the same technique over and over: different fruit juice, breakfast cereals, milkshakes, biscuits... I'll always remember the day when he made the decision about his favourite cheese. Again, we'd set it up as an experiment, and Dom was excitedly blindfolded. He'd placed the Cheddar in his mouth. He was accustomed to that, and to Lancashire, and they both received a thumbs up and high points rating. But he'd previously refused to try any of the others. Interestingly, the texture of Brie (my favourite) had made him retch and nearly abandon the experiment. It scored a zero for taste and a minus 1 for texture. Cheddar with walnuts looked to be the clear winner till he reached the final chunk - plain Stilton. He placed it into his mouth, grimaced, shook, flapped his hands and asked for a large glass of milk. We passed him the drink - what he called the 'cheese control' - and he washed away the spicy cheese taste. 'Can I have some more?' he asked. 'That was brilliant. First place.'

As a result of what he taught me during his taste tests, I myself began choosing something new and unusual every time I visited the supermarket. I began trying anchovies, green soya beans, Pop Tarts, wheatgrass... I didn't close my mind to new taste experiences any longer because if Dom could do it, so could I.

work

The day following Maggie's diagnosis saw me in work at 6am, and more than usually restless. Mark, my ex, was being a pain, and the reality of Maggie's condition was kicking in. I'd already decided how I could best help. It meant doing some more investigating on my own - and presenting her with the results.

Arriving earlier than usual, and earlier than the rest of my office team, I'd managed to plonk myself down at the only office desk whose monitor faced away from the door. This small advantage of hot-desking is only accessible if you're the first one in the office. It gave me freedom to check the internet.

Fortunately, my job was research-based. I helped struggling families to access facilities, discover routes to recovery they hadn't previously considered - that kind of thing. I looked for placements. I identified health needs.

By the end of the day I had downloaded eight care home options for Maggie to consider. I'd even booked a viewing at one of them, in addition to having completed a full day's caseload of work. I was the first to arrive and was the last to leave, with the exception of the cleaning staff. I said goodbye as this chatty group dragged their buckets of dusters towards my desk, and as I left I switched my on mobile phone.

Sixteen texts from Mark pinged their way into my consciousness. He knew I was not allowed to check my phone at the desk, and he also knew that I always left it switched off at work. 'Just leaving,' I wrote, and turned it off again. Positivity bubble popped.

Sluggishly, I walked to the car park where my Honda stood alone: apart from one other, parked deliberately adjacent to it. I was then that I silently thanked God for summer-lit evenings, because the other car was *his* car. I shivered and pulled my cardigan more securely onto my shoulders. It was *his* car and *he* was in it.

The window was wound down. His face was framed by the silver grey door, and my legs buckled a little under me. It was like looking at a face on the FBI's Ten Most Wanted poster.

'Get in,' he said as I drew alongside it. 'Leave your car here. You can get the bus tomorrow.'

I got in.

'That's a good girl,' he said as I walked round to the passenger door. As I sat, he removed the sheaf of internet research notes from my clutching fingers, glanced through them and threw them onto the back seat.

Then he held his hand up: it was a signal I knew very well. It meant NO FURTHER CONVERSATION.

dreams of the past

I finally escaped from him, exhausted and demoralised, at about 8pm. Even though we haven't been together for years, he still does this every now and again. I'm guessing he's trying to keep his hand in with his ex, just until he finds another woman to victimise full-time.

I rang Maggie's doorbell, and, as usual, I heard Dom's booming voice. 'Mum, the doorbell rang.' Maggie let me in, looking even worse than she had when I'd left her the previous day.

'I had a bad dream and it's worn me out all day,' she said as soon as the door was closed. 'Do you remember I always used to have them, especially when Dominic was still at school?'

Oh yes, I remembered those dreams and how those anxiety-ridden, graphic and terrifying imaginings had affected her. 'So I put Dom to bed an hour ago and came down here to try and catch up a bit on the sofa.'

'Oh, love,' I said. 'Not good for your aches and pains, I'm guessing.'

'I shake a little too much to sleep well anyway,' she said, looking away from me.

Back in her early days, Maggie had been reckless and outrageous. Yes, for a little while she'd experimented with bravery, till life's drudging normality caught her in its grasp. Back in those early days she'd lived in a damp and poky cottage in a small Yorkshire hamlet. It was a dreary place but it was only round the corner from me, so we had all loved its convenience. Anyway, it wasn't dreary when Mags and Dom lived there.

Nobody knows who Dom's Dad was - not even Maggie. It was just one of those 1970s party things.

We've all done it - taken risks - and everyone said that Mags was just unlucky. But sometimes I wonder about that. Perhaps she was the lucky one, because Mags had a life's mission. She was lucky because her life had become Dom and Maggie.

And back then, in the new house, domesticity prevailed. It was a completely unsuitable place for a child to be brought up, but back then the safety factors didn't seem to matter. And Maggie would go on and on about how much she enjoyed simple domestic pleasures like opening the tin of kit-e-kat for her mewing kitten, and how frustrating it was when she had to ask Dom to come downstairs for what must have been the 20th time.

I was there plenty. I'd help him with his boiled egg with cut-out zebra soldiers. And Dom would criticise my cutting and the ineptitude of my zebra shapes.

We'd always been big on honesty, the three of us, and on near-pointless, meandering conversations. They'd started when Mags and I would lie in our separate bunks and try to make each other giggle as we fell asleep. Oh, and the conversations - the madness of them! I taped one, sneakily on my hand-held recorder, when Dom was a little boy, and played it back a couple of years ago.

'You know the other day when I had to cancel our plans?' she'd said. 'Yeah,' I'd said. 'When I said I was tied up? With some DIY?' 'Yeah.' 'I said Kate had got me to install new lights?' 'Yeah.' 'And heating and all the rest of it?' 'Yeah.' 'Well, I got a bit of a problem.' 'Oh yeah,' I'd said. 'Yeah,' she'd replied. 'What is it?' I'd said. 'Well, you know how our kitten's a bit moody? A bit aggressive?' I hadn't noticed but went along with it. 'Yeah,' I said. 'Well, he bit me, bit Dom and bit Kate and then he bit into the lighting cable.' 'Bloody hell,' I'd said, wondering if this was going to become some elaborate joke, and if I should be either laughing, or if I should watch my back for cute but homicidal felines. But Maggie's stories, though typically dramatic in delivery, often went nowhere.

And Maggie reminded me of this every day: of how Dom is so literary and literal at the same time; and how he sees things more clearly yet also more darkly than the rest of us. How he has recently learned how to put the recycling in the bin and how to make cheese on toast, with supervision. That's the thing with him. Counselling, social care, support, he's had it all. It does help, but it takes time.

Maggie looked over at me. 'Are you ok?' she asked.

'I've been better,' I replied. 'It's Mark. He picked me up from work last night.'

'You're not...back with him?'

'No, we're not together. I never could go back to him, not after everything that's happened. But I know that's what he wants.'

'Well, of course he does! But you're not going to, are you?'

'I'm not!' I said, with renewed determination. 'That man is never coming near me again.'

'Me neither,' she said, as Dom edged into the room, shoulders clenched with fear.

'What's up, chick?' Maggie asked him. I have never seen her waver or lose patience when it comes to Dom.

'I've heard a noise. Outside. I think it was near the bins. It sounded like wolves howling, but I don't know. It could have been any number of things, but you know what? All of the things are bad. All of them are bad, Mum. All of them are bad.'

His arms flapped, hitting his stomach as he talked, and when he stopped he pressed them up against his face. If the problem couldn't see him, then he couldn't see the problem. Or was it the other way around?

'That's alright, sweets,' Maggie said, covering his hands with her own, till he gradually felt more confident to remove his own. 'I will go check for you,' she said, and Dom stood waiting till she returned.

'It's just the wind, honey,' Maggie said as she returned; her overactive hair providing visual proof of the gusts outside. 'Blowing the bin lids, and whistling up and down the gulley. Nothing to worry about. Really.'

Dominic nodded. Clearly his Mum's findings were acceptable to him, they being founded in logic and practical observation.

He left to go upstairs and we both watched him, blowing him ignored kisses, as we always have.

His bedroom door shut.

'What am I going to do about him?' Maggie asked.

I can't count how many times we've had this conversation, but it's happening more so recently, because it's getting increasingly obvious that things must change. And soon.

'I don't know,' I said, as I usually did. And honestly, I didn't, because I couldn't help more than I was already doing, and even then it didn't feel enough.

I had and still have problems of my own.

'These might help,' I said.

I handed Maggie the printouts I'd prepared and, silently, we went through them.

At almost ten o'clock I was ready to go home. My hair, usually brown-grey (who am I kidding, it's grey-white) was popping back into its damp usual ringlets every minute. Maggie's hair, poker straight, was long and white and lank.

We'd made progress - of sorts. Maggie had circled some phone numbers on the sheets I'd printed out, and was ready to make some calls in the morning once Dom was at his day centre. We already had one appointment booked via email, and she'd enthusiastically scored through others which didn't have the right feel, leaving the remaining places packed into a folder. She thanked me as she saw me off.

i need to tell you something

The following night, Maggie clearly had something other than care homes on her mind.

'I need to tell you something,' she said.

The way she spoke, the way she held her head, her facial expression, the way she played with the ends of her hair - it was clear that this all meant something to her: a whole lot of something. She'd spoken in that same tone when she'd finally admitted she was becoming unwell and asked me to accompany her to hospital.

'You know I love Mum and Dad to bits?'

I nodded. Of course I did. It hadn't needed to be said.

'Well, I'm going to try and find my family. My pre-adoption family.'

It was something I'd never considered. Surely she was happy as she was? Surely you didn't need to search for someone who had never wanted you? Could there be any benefit in doing so?

'What's brought this on?'

She sighed and tucked both floppy bits of white hair behind her ears. It was funny how we both had the genes to go grey early. It was one of the very few things we physically had in common. I stared at her hair, soft and velvety, and I longed to brush it as I had in the old days when we'd shared a bedroom. My hair was manic - curled and ringletted and untamed. Hers was thick and long and so good to brush.

'I've been thinking about it since I had Dom. Remember Irene, that woman who lived next door to us? Remember that as soon as she found out I was pregnant she called me all kinds of names for weeks and when it started to show she refused to speak to me? She told Mum and Dad that you could never tell what kind of child you'd end up with when you adopted. She said it was a risk and that it was almost inevitable I'd turn out bad. She meant well, but...'

Maggie's eyes teared up with the memory, but she continued.

'And she was so determined that I had to put the baby up for adoption to save my parents the shame of living with a teenage mother. But they weren't ashamed; they were just a bit shocked. We all were. And remember that you were in your final year of school and all the kids were teasing you about me? You got bullied on my behalf, and still I refused to abort. I wanted to keep him even before I knew he was a he, and what life with a baby was like. And when he was born I would have run away with him to protect him and be with him? Remember?'

I nodded.

She took a deep breath.

'I want to know why my parents didn't feel the same about me. I know that *our* parents did, but what about *mine*? I need to know, before I go. Before my health declines and it's too late for me. I need to know who they were and what happened - and I need to know if it was my fault.'

I nodded again.

'Will you help me, please?' she asked. There was no need. She knew I would. In reply, I hugged my sister tight. I hugged her because she will always be my sister, no matter what happens with her 'other' family. No matter what.

'Love you, Mags,' I said, letting go of the hug. 'We'll think about how to do it tomorrow.'

She grinned, a sad smile in a face pale, tired and troubled. 'Love you right back,' she said.

And when I left, fussing with my coat's hood to protect myself from rain while walking down their long driveway and into my car, I almost tripped over the white painted wheelbarrow stuffed with summer flowers. 'Pretty that,' I said, awkwardly to no-one, as Maggie closed the door.

Half way down the driveway I looked up, as I always did, to see Dom, a six foot ghost, hovering at his bedroom window, impassive and spectral. I love him intensely, but I didn't wave. He didn't either. That's not how it works.

the road to sheffield

We had somewhere to go, and had precisely six hours to get there and back while Dom was at his activity group. The arrangement was to drive over to Sheffield to investigate the first on my list of care places for Dom. Sadly, we were looking for a place for Maggie too. For obvious reasons, though I love them both more than my own life, they can't come to me. How I wish they could, but it's impossible, and Maggie knows it.

We've always been Radio 4 fans in our family. We were brought up on it, I suppose. Amongst our earliest memories: the crackling of a portable radio's tones in the family bathroom, especially on weekend mornings when Dad would go in to shave and shower, revelling in peace before the chaotic house woke. The theme music signalling the start of each programme became our weekend alarm clocks.

Ours was such a loving family: a family which I happened into quite accidentally when one sperm met one egg - a lucky chance for me.

But Maggie was chosen: selected as a babe in a cot from a council care home. Ironic that Maggie might soon be on her way back to a very different type of council home.

We'd been told the tale so many times. Mum and Dad, young then and the apprehensive, prospective parents of a preformed baby, were excited and sweaty-palmed as they held her. 'Is she really... ours?' my Mum had whispered as she had carried Maggie to their car, afraid to put her down in the second-hand navy blue carry cot for fear of breaking the spell.

A few months later, perhaps triggered by the hormonal madness that caring for a new born can instigate, this previously infertile couple realised that they clearly weren't barren at all. And then, there was me.

Only eleven months apart, Maggie and I were also about the same height and build - though Maggie always was a little heavier on the hips; and me on the tummy area: pears and apples; apples and pears.

And, though our faces were never really alike, we were definitely sisters under the skin.

My Uncle Arthur, Dad's brother, had been surprised that Mum and Dad had kept Maggie once they discovered they were expecting me. 'Surely you'll send the other one back now you're expecting a real kid of your own?' he'd said. My Dad still tells how he stood up to his brother for the first time in his life and stated, loud and proud: 'Arthur, you know nothing. Maggie is our own child and always will be. Being a parent isn't about genetics, it's about love'.

We listened to our usual Radio 4 and, as expected, we were inundated with a deluge of miserable news - suffering, illness, death, war and politics.

'It's all bloody doom and gloom,' Maggie said, then 'I've had enough of all that crap'. So, while I negotiated the M6, she messed with the DAB radio buttons till she found something suitable, never stopping for long on any one station (she was the same as a kid - never satisfied, and always looking for something better).

Then, when she'd found a station she was happy with, she slapped her thighs with satisfaction. It was such an odd gesture, but I don't think I was the only one to notice that such idiosyncrasies were coming to the fore recently.

About 20 miles from Sheffield she found a channel playing some terrible R&B track. Maggie has always loved this stuff and I accept that, but it wormed its way into my irritable psyche far too much. I felt sick down to the being of my soul and only just managed to drive as I tried to ignore Maggie's head and feet dancing in her seat.

I just kept my eyes straight ahead on the wet, black motorway. It might have been August, but that day was a dark-as-deep-winter-day, as the rain delivered a perpetual sermon of motion. The A-roads were no easier, despite their protection of lower speed. We were clearly close.

'Almost there,' Maggie said, trying to turn off the satnav before it annoyed her by telling her we'd arrived. Dom would have done just the same, had he been my passenger, and the thought made me warm inside. That baby, that kid, that man. I adored him.

'Not sure about this,' Maggie said, as she looked out through the side window once the car shuddered to a stop. She had a point. Red brick, huge, towering buildings weren't what Dom was accustomed to. They weren't what any of us was accustomed to. Maggie looked scared, but we didn't come all this way to go back home again. 'It threatens me,' she said, and I wanted to contradict her, but I couldn't. I knew it did, because it threatened me too.

But one of us had to be tough, and that person had to be me: just as it always was me, and pretty much always would be me. 'Come on, love,' I said. 'Even if we rule it out completely it's worth going in - even if it's just to see how awful it is! It'll be something to compare all the other great places with, like a benchmark.' Mags smiled, wanly, but allowed me to support her up the still wet steps to the gate.

Immediately we stepped into the grounds I realised that the care home was modelled on one of those huge red brick Victorian asylums. 'God, look at the size of it,' Maggie said. 'He'll lose himself in there.'

And I knew that, without me to guide and support her, Maggie would have turned round and gone back home. But I pushed it. I insisted. We pressed the buzzer. Correction: I pressed the buzzer as Maggie's fingers were shaking and we entered the building when the voice at the other end of the buzzer told us to push the door open after the click. It was calm on the outside, quiet even, but as soon as that huge, heavy door opened, we were straining to hear as Mr Thomasson bounded from the reception office to welcome us and tell us in excited tones how 50 men lived in this ex-stately home, and were cared for by the same number of staff.

'Gosh,' I said, warming even less to this army barracks of a place.

Maggie asked about their leisure facilities, how the residents found calm, how bullying was dealt with, whether they had many days out, and what the qualifications of the medical team were. She asked with a face as blank as I'd ever seen, and when Mr Thomasson replied describing the place as like a small campus university, her face didn't change. 'Oh yes,' he'd said. 'There are a huge selection of activities for Dominic to get involved in, and a huge number of people to meet. Loads of fun to be had.' Maggie just stared at her feet.

We left shortly afterwards and drove home in silence. It was a few days later before we talked about it again.

mark

Of course I love my family. But Mark's jealousy of the relationship I have always had with Maggie and Dominic was one of the factors which led to the abuse he meted out. He's not part of my life anymore, so I find myself wondering at my reluctance to move in with Mags and Dom: or, better still, have them move in with me. There's plenty of room here, and plenty of garden for Dom. We could build a special chemistry shed for him too. I'm sure he'd love that. But I'm tainted and am not quite right: a little troubled, and a little dangerous. I'm fine in small doses, but there's too much wrong about me.

Maggie understands. She's seen me at my worst and at my best. She knows I will always help her, just as I know she would do what she could for me. And she's the only one who knows that, while I seem serene on the surface, what lies beneath is gargantuan and troubled and desperate. So much is wrong.

Even in his absence, Mark is one of the things.

But there's more to it than that.

I used to look at Maggie's life and, I'll be honest, I was a little jealous. She didn't own all the physical trappings of your standard middle-class existence, as I had. She didn't own a sweet little bungalow with sloping dormer, but she also didn't have the black dog that I had accompanying my every footfall. We were dark and light in those early days.

Maggie was happy and she had nothing but Dom. I didn't even have peace of mind back then. By the time I met Mark he acted as if I should be grateful that someone so eligible still wanted me, when I was nothing more than a prematurely middle-aged woman who was way past her sell-by date.

Over the years I would often look for signs that Mark had changed, but there were none to be found.

There was no way that Mark should be allowed within metres of me and within metres of Dominic. His theoretical dislike for kids was undoubted. And, though Dom was very much an adult with his own issues and agendas, he was and probably always would be a partly dependent adult, and Mark despised him for that.

Of course, Dom was capable of actions and activities of daily life. What he wasn't capable of was putting thought behind them. He would brush his teeth if Maggie told him to do so enough times, or if he was following a behaviour chart. But if he was left to his own devices, his teeth would remain unclean.

Likewise, he knew how to cook basic foods and how to heat up canned items, but he didn't always know how to turn off the oven, or even that he was hungry. He'd assume hunger was anger, or say he only wanted a silky top that day, because the silk was happy – and that 'weirdness' would make Mark would tut and lash out.

The same happened around food. Dom would require ten chips on his plate. Nine was a bad number, and eight and eleven were tricky too, so if there was a number more or less than ten, he would not eat anything from his plate. Once presented with a plate of ten chips, each hand would select a similar sized chip and he'd put them in his mouth together. He'd do the same with the next two and the next two, till all ten were gone. Mark's reaction had been to add an additional chip underneath Dom's pork chop, which completely threw him at the end, and left him struggling to trust all of us, as he assumed we'd all been in on the 'trick'.

Again, food issues. Dom was a salad lover, but if there was the tiniest bit of dressing on his salad he wouldn't eat a mouthful, so Mark insisted on including dressing on every salad served to Dom.

Dom loved desserts but cheesecake would make him vomit even before he put it into his mouth, so Mark regularly brought cheesecake for Maggie, pretending he 'forgot' about Dom's preferences.

I think, more than anything, that Mark hated the thought of dependents. People were useful to you, or they were disregarded, but Dom would need some care forever. Even the prospect of Dom shopping on his own for everyday groceries was scary. One time when I took him to the supermarket, he calculated the total of the groceries without any effort whatsoever. Yet when we entered the local Co-op and I'd asked him what he felt like eating for his dinner, he looked into the trolley and simply said 'Some food'. I felt compelled to encourage him to consider it a little more. He shrugged his shoulders in that seemingly nonchalant way he had when thoughts were too big to think.

'If you were trolley master, what would you buy?' he asked me.

'Oh, all kinds of things. I'd buy chicken and salad and vegetables and juice. Perhaps some cake and biscuits and some good tea or coffee.'

'Let's buy chicken and salad and vegetables and juice and cake and good tea or coffee.'

'Okey dokey,' I said.

I couldn't love him more if he'd been my own.

Of course, I didn't have my own children. I came close once or twice with Mark, but once, when I was four months gone with our first child, Mark locked me in the bathroom for three days and nights and I miscarried from sheer terror and cold.

It wasn't an accident either. It was planned and considered carefully in advance.

The house we lived in back then was a red brick 1920s terrace. It had high ceilings and small rooms, and had been built with only an outside toilet. When, sometime in the 1970s, the bathroom had been installed, it was lovingly decorated with dark orange walls - all the better to complement its magenta bathroom suite. Much later on an electric fan was attached to the light pull switch. That bathroom was the only room in the house that had been cobbled together at the last minute. Being a mid-terrace and given that the bathroom was conveniently (and darkly) situated between the front bedroom and the back bedroom, it was the only room without a single window. And the only room with both an interior and exterior lock.

Once Mark had got me in there, he turned off the heating and boiler, so I kept myself alive by drinking from the tap and wrapping myself and my bump in towels from the freezing cold airing cupboard. I slept on that floor, with its rough prickly office-style carpet, for three nights, and the only joy I experienced was that my captor could not use the house's only bathroom.

When Mark came to release me in the morning after my third night, he found me in a crimson pool. Our baby was gone and I was blue, having given up the fight. In doing so I had seemingly also forfeited the right to be a mother. I should have shouted and screamed and broken down the door but I was anaemic and weak and my blood pressure was too low. I had no chance, and neither did my baby.

Mark was taken into custody after I called a taxi to take myself into hospital and I finally told the truth of what had happened.

'What did you do to provoke him?' a burly police officer asked. After a meal, a shower and a fresh set of clothes I was recovered enough to fight back. 'Are you married?' I asked. 'Yes,' he said, flashing me his ring. 'What would your pregnant wife have to do to be locked without food in a windowless, heatless room for three days and nights?' 'I never would do that, whatever she did. What kind of person do you think I am?' he responded. I didn't need to say anything more.

Later, once my physical damage had healed a little, I had to undergo the battle of getting Mark out of my life. Bit by bit he had hammered at my self-esteem till there was little left. I was as weak as a new-born kitten, and was even institutionalised for a little while. By the time I got out, impatience had done the ridding for me and he was gone - for good, I'd hoped. But it hadn't been.

He was gone for five years. But then he kept coming back.

the bee-whisperer

Maggie's outdoor chairs were green plastic, rickety and uncomfortable, but if Dom wanted to be in the garden he needed watching - and I needed to sit down. It wasn't that Dom couldn't be trusted, but inside felt safe to him. Outside didn't always.

I sat on the less bendy of the chairs, facing my nephew who was kneeling in front of a purple-pink snapdragon and holding our his hands to stroke it: calm, patient and beautiful. Seeing him like this it was hard to believe that his meltdowns could shake the floorboards with their intensity. But thankfully they were rare nowadays.

Dom seemed to have settled into a compromising alliance with the world. He accepted it, he accepted himself, and he had learnt, most of the time, to live within his limitations. I even think he might have been happy.

He certainly looked happy while snapdragon stroking. I walked over, eager to share his contentment.

He looked up. 'I like bees,' he said. 'Me too,' I said, accustomed to his random (to me) conversation, but as I moved in a little closer I realised that Dom was using his first two fingers to stroke a huge bumblebee resting within the snapdragon's flower.

'Does the bee like being stroked?' I asked. His fingers, strong and gentle and firm and precise, continued their hypnotic rhythm.

'Yes. The bee is a very social creature. It is drawn to activity and movement and when I stroke the bee it thinks I am its friend.'

'You're very gentle. How do you know you're not hurting it?'

'If I hurt the bee, it would fly away or sting me.'

His fingers stopped with the stroking. 'Look,' he said. The bee remained, almost purring with pleasure when Dom's fingers went back to it.

Maggie emerged from the back door with a couple of mugs of tea. Dom already had his bottle of lemonade. Though not surprised, I was a little disappointed in Maggie's offering. It was an early autumn weekend afternoon, the weather was bright and warm and we were sitting in her wild and overgrown garden. The least she could have done was to bring a bottle, and I certainly needed it after the few days I'd had.

Maggie had her own issues though - and that's what we were here to talk about: soberly. I forgave her the lack of wine, just as I'd forgive her absolutely everything. Dominic too.

'What are we going to do, then?' she asked as she laid the tea on the rickety green plastic table in front of my usual rickety green plastic chair.

'Dominic strokes bees,' I said, in a poor response. My sister looked at me for a minute and nodded her head. 'You can be as obtuse and random as Dom.'

'And that's why I'm his favourite auntie.'

'His only auntie.'

'That too.'

A brief pause.

'What are we going to do, Sally? Where do I start? About everything.'

'I'll help you, love,' I said. 'I've been thinking about it and I think we need to start with Mum and Dad.' Maggie's expression changed. Her mouth twitched expectantly. 'Won't they think I've let them down?' she asked. 'That I'm not grateful?'

'Of course not. We all know who and what you are. You're a brilliant, loving mum and a brilliant, loving daughter. I'm sure there's no requirement in the adoption contract that insists you have to show your special gratitude to them for taking you in off the street, by refusing to ever mention your past and never being anything other than perfect.'

'You think I try too hard to be perfect for them?'

'You do. It doesn't mean you're ungrateful or a cold, hard bitch, if you occasionally speak to them about your problems rather than sugar coating everything.'

Maggie suddenly reddened. 'I do not sugar coat everything and I can't believe you've even said that. All I do is to try my best for everyone and I don't deserve to get bitchiness in return.'

'Whoa Whoa Whoa,' I said, beginning to rise from my chair, not to punch her, but to get as much distance as I could between us before she punched me. I'd seen her like this before, and knew she was hurting more than she seemed willing to express in words.

'You always tell me to Whoa when I give you a little too much information or I show any feelings other than niceness, but then and you're the first one to tell me off for being overly nice and sugar coating everything. I'm never going to win, am I, not with Dom or with my health or with you… So I might as well just stop trying.'

'Don't stop trying. You're upset. You're sad and confused and you don't know which way to go next. You're overwhelmed, ill and angry at life and God for doing this to you.'

She shrugged. 'Great deductions, Miss Marple. So what else do you assume to know about me?'

'Size seven feet. Top half 18, bottom half 14, prefer silver over gold, prefer brown shoes over black. Did well at English and maths but could barely hold a ball for PE. Should I go on?'

Maggie smiled a reluctant little smile. 'I suppose you do know about me - a bit.'

'Yes, a bit, and I know you need to talk to Mum and Dad. Tell them your diagnosis and ask them the other question. You need to do it soon. Now would be a good time.'

She shut her eyes. Her lips twitched reluctantly.

'Or I could tell them?' I suggested. My role as the younger but stronger sister had rarely been questioned.

'No, I'll tell them,' she sniffed, brightening a little and opening her eyes to look at me, as if those few moments of darkness had granted strength. 'It's about time I did. And if a death sentence doesn't force me to grow up, I can't imagine what will.'

'When do you want to go?'

'Tomorrow morning. Sundays seem right for that kind of thing.'

I took a sip of my tea and turned back to Dom. 'He's been stroking that bee for at least fifteen minutes. I think it's put them both in a trance.'

'He's the bee whisperer,' Maggie said fondly. 'Maybe I should get him a bee circus and we could make some money out of it?' Her affection was real, but there was no hiding the anxiety behind her words. Telling Mum and Dad about her diagnosis was huge. She'd initially decided to tell them only when the symptoms were so obvious that there was no way of disguising them. I told her that wasn't good enough. She had to do it sooner - preferably today.

roots

Our parents had never been anything other than caring, loving and giving and had made no secret of how Maggie had arrived in the family. They'd been as proud of choosing her as she'd been proud of having been chosen. I wasn't left out: they used to say that they were proud I'd chosen them. We have a perfect family, they used to say. We could not be happier, they still say.

What Maggie doesn't know is that I'm already aware of how they will respond to her enquiry about tracing her roots. When I was in the final year of high school I was friendly with a girl, Becky, who was adopted, and whose parents weren't impressed when she'd told them she wanted to know more. So, while Mags was out, I'd asked our parents what they would do if she asked the same.

Dad had looked a little embarrassed. He was grey and balding even then, and hasn't changed much in the last thirty years. Mum, then black haired, but with the beginnings of worry lines, said, 'I fully expect her to ask and to want to know. We've a box up in the attic with all the details. We can give her addresses so she can find out more and we'll give her all the help she wants and needs'.

I'd been overwhelmed then, thinking of how shocked Maggie would be to find the answers already waiting, but I'd never told her of what Mum had said. I don't know why. Perhaps I was worried she'd go off and find another family who suddenly realised they had loved her all along, and then they would take her and Dom away from me.

I remember now how it had been only a few short months after that conversation with Mum and Dad, when Maggie had given birth to Dominic - in secret. Dominic was the result of a drunken one-night stand with a lad who'd gate-crashed a party. Mags had never been the same after that surprise birth, and it was Dom who took her away from me, not a historical link to her might-have-been past.

I had often considered my reticence over the years and wondered if Maggie might be better off knowing what Mum had said. Would I be better telling her about the box and the photos and the addresses? When Dom was about eight, and while Mags wittered on about Dominic's day care drama class, I made my decision, and my decision was no.

Mags needed to do some things for herself - and my telling her at that point would imply some kind of complicity in deception: the deception of omission.

And now, I considered preparing Mum and Dad for Maggie's news, but no – it wasn't the thing to do - not this time. She'd need me to advocate later when illness overtook and she couldn't do what she'd been used to.

Right now, she *could* talk to them, so she should. I equated it with the elderly person who wishes they could still cartwheel. If each week of their life they'd continued to cartwheel, they'd have a chance of still being able to do it. But the cartwheel gradually disappeared from their list of abilities without them even realising.

'I'll go with you if you like. I'm not working. I'd like to be there if you want me there.'

'Where did that come from?' Maggie giggled. 'You've not been listening to a single thing I've said, have you?'

'Sorry. No, I haven't been listening. But I do think we should go to Mum and Dad's today - the sooner the better.'

The shorter the time that my sister was struggling to deal with this disabling anxiety, the better. She nodded. 'Dom,' she shouted. 'We're going to see Grandma and Granddad. Get your shoes on, ok?'

He jumped up, leaving his bee a furry, hypnotised statue, and walked into the house with a huge grin. 'Grandma and Granddad. Get your shoes on, ok?' he said over and over. He came back with two shoes, one a trainer and one his shiny Sunday best.

'Dom!' his Mum said sternly, teasing him with her fake anger. 'A pair of shoes. Two that match.'

And Dom smiled his tiny, knowing smile.

grandma and granddad

Dominic was now jumping up and down in tiny flapping actions just inside the back door. 'Grandma and Granddad,' he said over and over. When he was in repeat mode, the best thing to do was to get him out of it. Sometimes this was easy. Sometimes not easy at all.

Today I said, 'Dom, stealth mode' and he immediately stopped his chant. Dom loved stealth mode with a passion. Stealth mode meant even more to him than the tuna sandwiches on dense wholemeal bread that his grandmother was forced to make each time we went there. He required just tuna and black pepper, with no mayonnaise to bind the mix together, and to make it softer and smoother. Just bread, tuna and pepper.

It was the only tuna sandwich he would ever eat. In actual fact it was the only sandwich, and the only bread he would ever eat. So, while Maggie fussed over Dom's hair (she combing it one way and a cheeky Dom pushing it back in another) I phoned Mum to check she had the tuna and a freshly made loaf.

In the car, Dom was quiet other than occasionally checking with us that there would be a tuna sandwich waiting. We didn't talk much. Maggie was always like that when Dom and I were both around. Our three subjects of conversation now - Dom's future, Maggie's future, and Maggie's distant past, were kept from Dominic, waiting for just the right time to be allowed to emerge.

Twenty minutes later we had arrived, the whole journey having been in a comfortable silence punctuated only by Dom's occasional tuna comment, and my mild mannered swearing at people who can't drive and who choose to use the roads anyway – seemingly to display their crass lack of skill.

Mum and Dad still lived in the house where we'd grown up, and so much remained as we had known it throughout our childhoods, though the garden had succumbed to a substantial number of changes. Easy-care, low-prune shrubs and conifers had replaced the garden's usual bedding plants and bulbs, and in some ways the whole character of the place had been lost as a result - Dad's flowers had always been his coup de grace.

Their back garden had changed even more than the front. Neat rows of vegetable and fruit canes had been replaced by paving, and the large lawn, once trimmed weekly to within an inch of its existence, had been transformed into a wild flower area. I knew for a fact that this was Mum's idea as she always did hate the sound of mowers ruining her summer days.

Inside the house much remained the same. The stairlift (or, as Dom called it, the 'stair chair') and an easy access bath were the only features that had been added.

We arrived at the front door and Maggie turned to me. 'Sal, I don't think I can do it. I think you may have to help a bit. Start me off, please.' I nodded. I'd been expecting it. She was my sister and I loved her.

Dom was already knocking, enthusiastic for food. The door opened. He said 'Grandma thank you,' and walked off, taking the tuna sandwich she'd brought to the door, as per their routine.

We walked into the living room of thrice-covered priory furniture and tile top coffee table, and Dad was in his usual armchair reading The Guardian. He glanced over the headlines at us as we entered. 'Well, well, well,' he said. 'We'd given you all up for dead!' Another statement as per routine. Dom giggled from his seat on the sofa. It was the same seat he always sat in, and the same giggle he always did.

'So, girls, to what do we owe the honour of your visit?'

In Maggie's face, a pale panicking began. She nodded and I knew what she wanted from me.

I gulped and began.

secret's out

'Can I have a chat, love?' asked Dad, once we'd dealt with Maggie's business. He looked unusually shy and uncomfortable: even worried, or uneasy. I couldn't quite tell.

'Of course,' I said. We left Maggie and Mum to examining the box of adoption information and Dad took me into the kitchen, guiding me with his hand on my back. Once we were in and the door was closed, he cleared his throat and invited me to sit. I refused, not liking how their dated rattan work seats gave my thighs dimples.

'We know more than your mum has told Maggie, Sal. We know more about Maggie's mum. She died of the thing that Maggie's got. That's why she gave her baby away. She had been hoping for a baby for years, but by the time she conceived it was too late. Much too late. And now I don't know how to tell Maggie. If she's going to try and find her, she won't find her. She's been dead a fair few years now.'

My dad sighed and held on to the back of a chair for support. 'She's so excited, but I know she has to know. What should we do?'

And, as ever, Sally came to the rescue.

'I'll tell her,' I said. 'Don't worry, I'll tell her.'

the journey

'Do you know what I was just talking about?' Maggie asked.

'Not sure. Perhaps Dom?' I guessed. And my sister laughed so much that the car seat shook and her poor little eyes were red with glee.

'What?'

'I was talking about bus fares back when we were kids!' I shrugged. The roads and motorways so far had been clear but traffic was fast-moving and just right for accidental accidents. I had to stay on my guard. It was a long journey to Scotland.

Her body shook as she pushed her hair roughly behind her ear. Not only did I not know what she was talking about, but I couldn't remember what we'd been talking about for the entire journey till now. My mind is beginning to let me down. Mind, memory, consistency, all of it. I find myself getting more tired too. My doctor says it isn't surprising given everything I've been through, but I don't think it's quite as simple as that.

I always liked to stop pretty much at the half way point of every long journey to have a full meal. I'd checked online, and the halfway point for this journey was a service station called Medbank. It was safe, it was less than 30 seconds off the motorway, and it was clean and bright.

'I want to go somewhere else,' said Maggie. 'I'm not spending my only holiday for three years eating in a motorway service station.'

She had a point, but this place was a transit stop, that was all. We were simply on the route to our destination. We'd have plenty of time to eat, drink and holiday once we arrived.

'I'm not eating at a soul-less service station. I don't care how clean or convenient it is. I'm just not. Let's take the next turn off this road and find ourselves a pub or a cafe.'

'No,' I insisted. 'It's on the plan to go to Medbank.'

'Who do you think you are,' she countered. 'Dominic?'

I winced. This woman, my sister, never took her son's name in vain. She never would use him as a comparative insult.

'Sorry, Mags. We're going here, or we won't have time to check out other pubs and hotels before checking into the one I've booked.'

'And why do we even need to do that? Let's just have a good lunch in a nice place. It's getting late for lunch now.'

I sighed, and knew this was a battle I wasn't going to win. She was right. The car's clock said 2:35 and we were behind schedule. Roadworks twenty miles back had held us up. And Mags was right – we needed to eat and I needed a bit of a break. Without food we were becoming grouchy.

It had been pushed to the back of my mind, but I still remembered vividly how Mark had hated my grouchiness, and when Maggie argued with me. He wasn't protective of me (how silly to even think he might be). It's more that he was jealous of Dom and Mags and the power they had over me. How I always wanted to make things right.

Schedules were such ridiculous constraints. Why did I need a schedule to tell me where to eat and when? I must be as mad as Mark claimed.

I turned to Maggie and, hands gripping the steering wheel tight, said, 'I'm sorry. We'll do as you say'.

We stopped at the first pub we found and by the time we finished the meal (an extremely commonplace cod, chips and peas) the atmosphere between us had settled a little.

And, by the time our journey ended - a journey that had begun loudly, excitedly and with much expectation, all was normal.

'We don't need to look for anywhere else. Let's just stay here,' Maggie said, as we pulled up into the car park at Cobblestones. 'It's perfect.' I opened the glove compartment and, without checking the screen, put my phone in.

Yes, Cobblestones would do. It was handy too. We were just across the road from the house where Maggie's 'birth uncle' lived.

We checked in, showered and got into our nightclothes then I sneaked down in my dressing gown to order us a couple of Irish coffees. We each lay in our adjacent beds in our delightful loft room, sipped our drinks (thankfully caffeine before bedtime had never caused any sleeplessness for either of us), watched some documentary about the navy in the Second World War, and both waited to gradually drift off to sleep. It had been a long and exciting day.

Maggie glanced over at me and raised her eyes, her brow crinkling just like Dom's as she did so.

'You want to go home, don't you?' she said.

'You know me. The second I've got over the trauma of having unpacked, I'm ready for leaving again.'

'Since the age of five. I remember that holiday in Northumberland very well. You adamantly refused to have fun for 13 full days. That was a holiday and a half.'

'Yes, that really was a holiday and a half. Remember how everyone kept saying I was miserable? I wasn't miserable at all. I was enjoying it, if I remember rightly, but that didn't stop me wanting to go home.'

'I'd try to get you to play or swim - do you remember - but all you would do was stare into the distance and whine. Very like Dom at age five, actually.'

'Me and Dom are a lot alike. For a start, both of us are totally aggravated by you.' She reached over and pinched my upper arm through the duvet.

'We'll be alright,' she said.

cobblestones

Cobblestones was delightful. It was a pretty, whitewashed pub conveniently situated none-too coincidentally, just over the narrow road from Andrew's house. Andrew was the eldest brother of Morag, Maggie's birth mother, and it was him we were here to see.

The room was attractive, with patchwork quilts on both beds and pretty pastel tones on the walls, and the staff members we met were all exceptionally friendly and polite. We'd both slept well in our unusually comfortable beds, covered with snuggly goose-down duvets, and what felt like thick Egyptian cotton sheets. Though we were getting a lot for our money, I still would have rather been at home under my own unremarkable duvet in my own unremarkable room, instead of being about to embark on this simple but terrifying quest.

But it's good I'm here. It's all about Maggie, and that means there's no time left for me. That's the way I like it, because when I do get time alone, the demons arrive: the smell of giving up, the feelings of dread, and the devastation of lying in a bathroom, covered in blood.

Fear of living, fear of dying, fear of half-life where the living's worse than the dying ever could be. Fear of food, of relaxation and of fear itself. Whatever you do isn't good enough, isn't strong enough, isn't kind enough, isn't wild enough…

This was how it was with Mark. And I know it's like this again because he's back. The most worrying thing is that I don't know why.

Showered and dressed, it wasn't long before we had settled into the breakfast area of Cobblestones, and were offered tea, coffee, toast, a cooked breakfast, or scrambled eggs and smoked haddock. I chose the fish. Maggie, always making the most of every meal she didn't have to prepare herself, went for the full cooked meal with bacon, eggs, square flat sausage, eggs, mushroom, cooked tomatoes and a couple of dessert spoons of haggis on the side. 'Mmm, you're missing a treat here,' she said.

'Mine's good too.' Breakfast was delicious, though the dining room was unlike any I'd ever seen before – it being packed with mirrors and unusual artwork, taxidermy experiments and beer or whiskey promotional goods.

Full of food, we left by the front door and admired the pub's twee exterior, with bulging whitewashed walls and its tiny windows each with a hand-made red-painted window box. Each window box was stuffed full of geraniums, though the odd comforting dandelion and daisy wildly rebelled amongst the prim and proper cultivars. A good night's sleep and a decent breakfast had set us up for our wander along to the tourist information office. We bought a map and sat outside Cobblestones with a pot of tea each. We looked at the map. And we watched number 85.

And that was how we spent much of our time at Cobblestones. I grew to love, and at the same time, hate the contours of this quaint little road and the frontage of number 85.

It was Tuesday. We'd been at Cobblestones since Saturday evening, and we'd seen nothing of the person we came to see. The door knocks remained unanswered.

Maggie picked up her ringing phone for the third time that day. It was Dominic. He was having a miserable time and wanted to come home. How alike we were.

He also wanted his mum to come home, and I wondered, not for the first time, if he might have contrived sadness in order to connect with her.

He couldn't just ring her and say he'd missed her. He had to make something happen. Pretend a reason.

As Dominic and Maggie chatted, she comforting, consoling, and supportive - as ever - I looked up to see a middle-aged man, or perhaps old man, with white fluffy hair and a tweed overcoat, opening the door of number 85 with a key.

We had worked out that Andrew must be about 65. It could have been him. I nudged Maggie who looked up at me.

'What, Sally? I'm talking to Dom,' but when she followed my glance and read my lips saying 'Andrew,' she told Dom she had to leave. 'That was him?' she said.

'It was him.'

We finished our drinks, slowly and deliberately, and I waited for Maggie to stand up. 'I'm wobbly,' she said. Nerves. Illness. Whatever it was, she was not quite ready to take control. Sally to the rescue.

'I'll go,' I said.

'No, no, no… I've got to come too. I've got things to give him.'

Nervously, we both rose. This was why we'd come all this way. This was why Dominic was struggling along in respite care for a week. This was why we'd spent the last three days sitting and staring at number 85. 'I don't know if I can do it,' she said. I grabbed her arm, and we began to walk, purposefully, the few metres across the road.

I knocked, as there was no bell. I probably knocked a few too many times as he arrived at the door, hair windswept, and face grumpy.

'Hello,' I said.

'Lo,' he mumbled, looking suspiciously at these two white haired middle-aged English women who had suddenly appeared on his doorstep. And suddenly, and unusually for me, I just dried up.

Maggie tugged at my sleeve, but I had frozen.

'What do you want?' he asked with a well-practised frown. 'I'm away to my tea.'

Maggie cleared her throat. 'Hello. You are Andrew Kilbright?'

'I am. And whatever you're selling, I don't want it.'

He glared at me as if I was a debt collector.

'So, who are you?' he said, to us both.

Maggie leant on me for support again and began playing with her hair. 'I'm Maggie, and this is Sally, my adopted sister. Your sister Morag was my mother.'

She'd said it.

'Oh, so that's it,' Andrew said. 'That's it.'

'I was hoping we could come in and ask you a few questions,' Maggie continued.

'No, you can't. Morag didn't have a child called Maggie. You've got it wrong.'

Andrew made to close the door, but I stuck my foot in. 'You see, Andrew, we have all this information that proves she did have a daughter. Maggie doesn't want anything from you. She just wants to talk. Please could she come in for a moment? Or we could meet you in a few minutes at the Cobblestones. We'll get you a drink. Some food?'

My sentence tailed off. Andrew's face was reddening.

'I know you don't believe me,' said Maggie, 'but please could you just take these and look at them. We'll call again.'

'Aye, aye,' he said impatiently, grabbing the bulky brown envelope from Maggie.

'Can you see a likeness, Andrew?' I asked. 'Does Maggie look like your sister?'

'Aye, maybe,' he said. The door was practically slammed behind him, leaving the pair of us standing on the path.

Inside the envelope were copies of Maggie's birth certificate, photographs of her and our family over the years (including a few of Dominic), a copy of the adoption letters that Mum and Dad gave her, and a personal letter for the attention of Andrew himself. I'd read the letter the previous night.

"Dear Andrew,

I am sorry that my sister and I are intruding on your life. Genuinely, we mean no harm. I just need to let you know that your sister, Morag, was my mother. I don't know why I was put up for adoption, but I don't blame her for what happened.

I would just like to know more about her. You see, I'm ill and don't know how much longer I'll be around. But I don't want anything from you, other than the answers to a couple of questions. Please could you ring me? My number is at the bottom of the letter. I'm in the area till Friday. This might be the final opportunity I get to be here. I don't want to make you feel guilty if you aren't able to see me, but please look through the contents of the envelope.

45

Please, for my sake and Dominic's, and Morag's. Thank you, from Maggie."

Maggie and I turned away from number 85 and trudged slowly back to Cobblestones. We weren't surprised at Andrew's reaction, but I know that both of us had been hoping for a little better. Instead of feeling small and rejected on our journey back to our rooms, we had hoped be settled in Andrew's sitting room listening to tales of Morag and the family.

Even the brief number of footfalls back to the pub allowed a dark, heavy mist from the sea rain to descend over us. The moisture frizzed up my hair, and reduced us both to silent, mutual tears.

what to do about andrew

'What do we do now?' Maggie asked me, as I returned from the bar with our order of tea and scones.

She was staring out of the window directly at Andrew's home.

'I guess we just have to give him some time to read everything. Perhaps make a few phone calls, check a few facts; that kind of thing.'

'Do you think he will?' Maggie asked anxiously.

I could tell that she didn't believe he would - not for a minute. Hope had been crushed into apathy, and she'd already mumbled to me about the visit not being worth it. Andrew was down on the adoption forms as Morag's next of kin, and fortunately was still living at the same address. That was why we came here. Without Andrew, we had nothing.

We sat in silence, both staring towards number 85. 'I ordered tea and scones,' I told her, but it barely registered. We drank the tea when it arrived. We spread the scones with jam and ate them, though without much enthusiasm. We stared for the next two hours until the lights went on at number 85.

'At least he didn't escape out the back door,' said Maggie.

We ate our evening meal, not having left the table and both staring alternately and expectantly at number 85 and at Maggie's tiny red Nokia.

I ordered a double whisky each. We drank in silence, but as we finished our drinks, the lights went off at number 85.

'I'm going up to bed,' Maggie said.

indian summer

Early next morning the sun swarmed in through the windows. 'Scottish Autumn,' I said yawning. 'Indian Summer,' Maggie agreed, coughing and accepting the cup of tea I handed her. Her arms shook with the effort. 'I must do something with my hair,' I said. 'Look at the state of it.'

She smoothed her own. 'Mine's a little salty. Bagsy first shower.'

The honeysuckle wallpaper adorning this bedroom was echoed in Maggie's heady honeysuckle and almond soap. Her defining scent.

As Maggie got dressed and I made my way towards the bathrooms rich, sweet, soapy smell, I shouted through to her - 'Let's have a day to ourselves and pretend we're on holiday. He's got our number.'

As she pondered this and I proceeded to shower, the phone's trilling echoed throughout our room, its ringing urgent and efficient and totally at odds with how the pair of us felt. Frozen to the spot I switched the shower off, though my hair was still covered in shampoo.

'Shall I answer it? I don't recognise the number,' Maggie said.

'Do it.'

Maggie picked up the receiver. 'Hello,' she said - her voice shaky with sleep and anticipation. The voice on the other end of the phone left her face changed. 'It's Dom,' she said. 'He's calling from the phone of a new friend – his has run out of battery.'

I turned the shower back on and jumped about a bit waiting for it to warm up. I rinsed, dried myself, dressed in the bathroom and returned to our bedroom just as Maggie's phone conversation was ending. I rearranged the silk freesias in the delicate glass vase between our beds as Maggie finished talking.

'See you soon then, Dom,' Maggie said. 'Love you loads.'

She clicked the button on her phone, Andrew having been forgotten just for a minute. 'How is he?' I asked, already knowing the answer because her face told Dom's story. 'He's settled in. He's fine. He's happy to stay. He just wanted me to know.'

We both knew how difficult respite care had been for him in the past. He'd spend his days in a conflict of emotions: missing, enjoying, scared and waiting. It seemed those days were gone –such strides he took, such changes.

It was breakfast time.

We sat together in pleasant silence with only the odd slurps of eating and drinking from the other breakfast guests, till Maggie's phone went, making us both jump. 'Is it him?' I asked. 'Dom again,' Maggie said, answering his ring.

'Hello honey,' she answered, getting up to move to the corridor. I sat in silence, finishing my meal, overhearing only the smallest snippets of their conversation. 'Badminton, not bagminton,' she corrected. 'Oh, a party,' she exclaimed, and 'Love you loads, Dom, see you in a couple of days'.

'He's loving it,' she said coming back into the room. 'I think I need a day of fun today. Like Dominic's having. I wonder what there is to be done round here.'

'There's a harbour,' I said. 'A fish stall. We could buy some fresh shrimps, like we used to as kids. There are some nice shops down the side street behind here. There's a woollen mill...'

I was interrupted by Maggie's exclamation, 'There's always a woollen mill'.

'Well, let's go buy some woolly jumpers then. There's a bookshop too - a couple of doors down from the woollen mill.'

'How do you know this stuff?' she asked.

'I checked online the night before we left.'

'You're a marvel.' There was no trace of irony or sarcasm in her voice. Maggie genuinely admired my organisational skills. To be honest I never paid them a second thought. She was the one who was to be admired, dealing with Dom all on her own.

She smiled at me. 'It was so good to hear from Dom. I might have given up on Andrew, but not on Dom. Never on Dom.'

'He's always got the power to surprise you, hasn't he?'

'He has. Always.'

Maggie looked away and took a sip of her drink, leaving a final few mouthfuls of her Full Scottish Breakfast on the plate, drowning under the weight of bean juice.

So, it was decided. We'd wander round the harbour, visit a couple of the cafes and a few of the more upmarket shops. And we would definitely visit the woollen mill.

Within half an hour we'd returned to our room and got ourselves ready for a day out. Ten minutes after that we were strolling round the grey-green harbour. Maggie's pocket securely held her mobile phone, turned to the highest volume.

The skies were clear on that perfect autumn day, and it really did feel as if we might be on holiday. The fish processing area was situated on the outskirts of the more touristy part of town, and we watched plastic pallets of fish and seafood were carried by wagon, by forklift, and by hand to a small seafood stall right by the harbour front. Just big enough for one or two people to stand inside to serve customers, this was the kind of place our parents had always frequented on holiday, and thus had become what Maggie and I had grown to love.

Maggie looked in admiration at the stall's blackboard menu. She had the look of someone whose breakfast had left a gap. The seafood stall had caught her eye.

'What are you getting?' I asked.

'Same as usual. Bag of shrimps, bag of steamed mussels and a bag of whelks.'

'For lunch? You've only just had breakfast.'

'It's my second breakfast,' Maggie replied with a huff. 'And I'm on holiday,' she insisted.

'Absolutely,' I agreed, for the sake of peace rather than for the sake of seafood. 'Same for me, then.'

And, noticing the sign on the stalls blackboard, I couldn't help myself.

'Ooh let's get a pile of scraps for the seals.'

We wandered over to the feeding station with arms full. The sign was badly painted with a terrible rendition of a seal: the poor creature was cross-eyed and dozy-looking. As we walked, each clutching our bags, we both picked daintily at our own seafood selections, perched on top of the larger paper bags of scraps. It had only been an hour since we'd finished breakfast. Perhaps it was the fault of the sea air, but I was definitely a little peckish.

At the edge we looked down to the platform where, gloriously, and fortunately for us, two huge adult seals lay basking, secure in the knowledge that they were safe and that food would come along soon - with minimal effort. They had good lives, those seals, and we greatly enjoyed the few minutes it took to throw the scraps into the water they'd come from just a few hours before, and watching the seals as both gobbled the piece up from the platform and dived in to retrieve the pieces that fell short.

'We're at the end of tourist season,' I observed. 'Those seals are probably stuffed.'

'Like me,' said Maggie with a cheeky grin, showing me her empty seafood bags. 'Better for me than any medicine.'

'I'll tell your consultant. Perhaps they'll start putting whelks on the NHS.'

andrew

We decided on half an hour in the woollen mill. I was going to purchase a silly souvenir for Dominic, and Maggie something new to wear. Walking just a little way from us was Andrew. He hadn't noticed us.

'Andrew,' Maggie shouted, instinctively. She hadn't intended it and reddened as he turned to face us and immediately recognised his caller. But he didn't walk over to us; instead he pulled his cap a little further down, turned around and continued walking away, in almost the opposite direction.

'Shall we follow him?' Maggie asked.

'No,' I answered. 'I think he just needs a bit more time'. Though there was no way of knowing if he'd ever come round to having a new niece, I needed to say something that would make Mags happier and keep her hopeful and calm.

'He doesn't need more time,' Maggie said. 'He needs a bloody personality transplant.'

So, I linked my arm through hers and we got on with enjoying our day. The day had undercurrents of upset but we made it count, in our own silly way. Maggie purchased a couple of new shirts, a new coat and a pair of slippers and a writing pad. I mainly followed behind her, enjoying her enthusiasm. This was Maggie's time: I had the rest of my life to shop.

By the time we got back to Cobblestones, some of the fire had gone from Maggie. I could read my sister like a book – and she was a damp and disappointed book that had been dropped in the bath and was drying, rough and crumpled, never to be the same again, on the laundry airer. I sighed deeply as we neared the final set of pub stairs to our room.

'Are you alright?' Maggie asked.

'Out of condition, that's all. Spend too much time sitting in front of a computer or in front of a family who need help.'

'Or sitting at my kitchen table complaining about Mark. What's going on with him anyway?' Maggie asked. 'I noticed you had a text from him last time you were round.'

'Oh yes. Were you checking up on me?'

'No. No, not at all. The phone went and I grabbed it thinking it was mine. Hoping it was you know who. Misery guts. Mark too. You need to tell him to sod off.'

How different things would be if I was here with Mark rather than with Maggie. He certainly wouldn't have tolerated my half hour conversation with the elderly lady in the woollen mill. I remembered how, while walking through our nearest town on market day, I'd chatted briefly to the woman on the vegetable stall as she bagged our selections. We'd been at school together, Carol and I, and hadn't seen each other for over twenty years.

'Why would you talk to a woman like that?' Mark had moaned afterwards.

'We were school friends. We were very close. And what do you mean, a woman like that? Like what?'

'A market trader.'

'Market traders are people, Mark, or hadn't you noticed?'

'No I hadn't,' he'd said. 'They might be people. But they aren't worth wasting five minutes of my time on. Don't do it again,' he demanded.

I'd decided way before this point that I didn't love Mark. He had something wrong within his very being.

He didn't have a brain processing disorder of the type Dom had. It wasn't even as simple to say that he had a different outlook on the world.

Underneath his prevailing surface humanity, Mark was empty. It was a veneer; just surface gloss.

Maggie. I should have listened to her when she said within two weeks of meeting him - 'Mark has the eyes of a psychopath'.

She wasn't wrong.

Out of loneliness, I bought a hamster and got her a huge cage: the biggest I could afford. I bought an old second hand aquarium too, and I'd let Beryl the Peril explore it and burrow in the sand and sawdust. 'You're a 34 year old woman,' Mark had moaned. 'Small, furry things are for children. Give it to Dominic. He'll never grow up.'

But I loved that hamster, especially when she'd fall asleep briefly in the excitement of burrowing, her bottom facing right up with her nose squashed on the base of the tank, when she fell asleep in her food bowl, half-way through nibbling on a seed or grain.

'She's a baby substitute,' he'd said. Well, maybe she was that. But three weeks after I bought Beryl, she was gone. One of the tubes was unattached from her cage and she had sneaked out in the night. Mark said she must have fallen as she clambered down from the table where I kept her digging tank and home.

The thing was - I knew Mark had done it.

What kind of a man would be insanely jealous of a creature not even big enough to fill his palm?

For months I'd look and listen out for signs of Beryl pulling up the edges of the carpet and using them as bedding, and I'd leave food and drink on the floor next to her open cage. I checked her bed every day for three months till I was finally convinced that she was truly gone.

I still have that cage now, in the loft. The lid is still open and the digging tank is still full of Beryl's sawdust.

But even Beryl's disappearance wasn't enough to give me the kick up the pants I needed to leave Mark. But it wasn't misplaced loyalty that was keeping me going. It was fear: plain and simple fear.

His wide face and far-apart eyes had a leonine look. He was a predator: a sociopathic predator, silently roaring his supremacy. Maggie had been right. I should have left when I had the chance. I should have moved away. Changed my name. But Mags and Dom needed me, just about as much as I needed them.

Have you ever had that feeling that life has carried you away, and that it has done so without the permission of logic? Well, that was me and Mark.

'Sally,' I heard Maggie say, 'You're awfully quiet. Everything alright? You're not letting Andrew's miserable sodness get you down, are you?'

'Just a little,' I replied as I pushed myself to move my thoughts back into the present day.

Safely through our bedroom door, we nursed our hands, sore and ridged with carrier bag marks. Maggie was quieter than usual, perhaps thinking her none-too-secret thoughts and wondering about Andrew. We lay each on our respective bed, and I was glad of the quiet.

losing that loving feeling

Mark had seemed to be a good man when we first met, but it didn't take long for him to lose that loving feeling. Odd, isn't it, how relationships rise and fall, and how feelings, no matter how illogical and pointless, have the power to completely blow you away with their intensity?

He certainly wasn't the greatest looking partner I'd ever had, not the most intelligent, and certainly not the kindest, but something seemed to click. I'd met him at a time in life when I'd assumed I would never be married or have children. I had accepted, and in fact embraced the prospect of a life which consisted of Dom, Maggie, my parents and work. I was happy, and I certainly wasn't desperate, but Mark must have sensed something available and pliable about me. The sociopath and the empath have an almost inevitable symbiosis.

He'd been working on the floor below me and had opened the door from the stairwell to admit me into his offices. I immediately noticed his pale blue shirt and charcoal pants, combining enticingly with his ash blonde hair.

His eyebrows raised as he saw me: as he looked me up and down.

I thanked him for opening the door as the folders in my arms were unsteady and liable to fall.

'You're welcome.'

Then, 'You work on the third, don't you?'

'I do,' I'd said.

'I'm on the second. Hopefully I'll see you around.'

After that, he made it pretty clear that he wanted to see me around more and more. Within a few weeks he was bringing me my lunchtime sandwiches. But it didn't take long for the loving feeling to fade.

andrew talks

We woke late and sat in the Cobblestones lounge for a leisurely breakfast. Again, we wandered to the harbour, and again we fed the seals. As they barked and splashed, we watched silently.

And at the same time, and in the same place as we saw him yesterday, Andrew appeared, but this time he didn't seem to be ignoring us. In fact, he was almost sheepish.

As he came closer he beckoned to Maggie and sat himself down on a metal bench, encouraging her to do the same. From his coat pocket, he pulled out a brown envelope and from inside he pulled out a copy of his sister's death certificate, which he passed to Maggie.

'She died of…?' she muttered as she read, nodding her head. 'I knew… but it's so much more real when you see…'

Andrew didn't engage in conversation. Instead, from deeper within the brown envelope he pulled out a handful of photographs.

'Your mother,' he said. 'You look a bit like her. You can keep them if you like.'

'Thank you,' Maggie whispered.

'I don't want to see you again,' said Andrew. 'I don't want the rest of the family to know about you. Just ask me what you need to know and then go.'

'I only have one question. Did she love me and want to keep me?'

Andrew scratched his rough chin with a dirty finger. 'Aye, I think she did, but she obviously couldn't with being poorly. There was only me that knew about you. So that was that.'

With a mock bow, he left us: Maggie still sitting, staring alternately at the death certificate in one hand, and a portrait of her birth mother in the other. I still standing, but now holding onto the waste bin for support.

Andrew's had given an incredibly unsatisfying answer to Maggie's question. But it was better than nothing, and was likely the best we were going to get.

realisation

Maggie remained on the bench for quite some time: mainly silent, and mainly still. I stayed where I'd been, unwilling to break the spell. Even when a young lad came over with his mum to carefully drop his lolly stick into the waste bin, I still remained holding its outer shell.

But my leg began to twitch and spasm (a longstanding problem) and I began to tire, so prised myself from the sticky bin and sat myself next to my sister, immediately removing the antibacterial wipes and tissues from my bag. The wipes were for my mucky hands, but I had a feeling that Maggie might need the tissues soon.

'She died of it,' Maggie said. 'She was young too. She died only a little while after I was born. That's why she gave me away.'

And then the tears of many years fell. Heavier and harder than I'd ever witnessed her tears fall.

I handed her the box of tissues.

decisions

We still had a couple of days left of our holiday, but there seemed no point in staying. Any hopes that Andrew might hold a huge party in Maggie's honour, and introduce her to the entire family, had completely faded. He had communicated with us the minimum that was required for human civility, but somehow neither of us could bring ourselves to hold it against him. He had done the best that he could do. And Maggie knew what she needed to know.

'Definitely leave today?' Maggie asked, already removing her toiletries from the shelf next to the sink and squeezing them into her wash bag.

'Might as well,' I said.

As we drove back down south, my mobile phone rang. I'd left it in my unused car the entire time we'd been in Scotland and its ring was unfamiliar and grating.

'Get it for me, would you?' I asked Maggie, pointing to the glove compartment.

'It's Mark,' she said. 'I'm going to text him,' she said, ignoring the call which turned out to be the 23rd since I'd left the car.

'Sally knows what you've done. Keep away from her or she goes to the police,' she texted.

'What are you talking about?' I asked as she read her text out to me.

'Andrew's not the only one who can keep secrets,' she said.

changes

Dominic's old bedroom had been ransacked in order to facilitate the person he aimed to become. His Doctor Who posters, his teddies and his Lego, all used and loved till quite recently, were left behind for me to package together and take to the charity shop.

Maggie's room was the same. The few items remaining, the peeling wallpaper, and a single dusty slipper might have served as a sad reminder that the rest of her life would be downshifted, smaller and more limited. But somehow, the items remaining don't convey that message to Maggie. Instead, they spoke of hope.

This is what we leave, she said.

How much better our future will be.

They had been offered places in adjacent independent living flats.

How much better...

Mags and Dom were fine at letting go.

However, there was an indefinable something holding me back. I knew that these moves needed to be made, but it was so hard to be ruthless and objective about their belongings and about these places they've always loved. Places I've loved too.

Dominic is unwilling to re-remember the piles of his possessions currently resting in charity shop donation bags, as he knows if he sees them again he will want them back. But wisdom hits us all, and he has suddenly come to a realisation that his wants do not always tally with his needs - and that, I believe, makes him future-proofed. Grown-up. Of course he *wants* it all, but now knows it is sometimes best to let go. This does not mean that I, his auntie, have let go of respect for what he owns. No - I clear his items, pack them carefully, ready for their new lives in charity shops, and make my fifteenth trip.

On my return I find Dom in the lounge, sitting on the corner of the sofa. It's the only furniture remaining, just waiting for the Craigslist lady to pick up.

I start as I realise that in Dom's hands is a well-thumbed letter. It is written on the same paper as was the letter Maggie wrote to Dominic on diagnosis day.

'May I?' I asked Dom. He shrugged and handed it over. I began to read.

"To the best boy ever,
Almost 38 years ago I gave birth to you. You would say 37 years, 50 weeks and 2 days or something like that. I'm less precise, as you know, but that doesn't mean that I don't remember.

My hospital gown was ripped. Just a tiny tear in that diaphonous medical clobber, but I remember these things. You would have too.

There was no encouragement back on September 7th, 1978 to give birth in water, or roll around on beachballs. You just turned up at hospital with your little bag and child's layette, and got on with it. On your back. Agonised.

And that's what I did. And there you were. Sweet as a button. Always were. Always will be. And that's why I can't trust myself to tell you this in person, because I know I won't see you make it to 40. I am unwell, Dom. I might just make it a little longer, but believe me, I won't be leaving you because I want to. I will fight this disease until I can't fight any more.

You asked me yesterday if I was sad, and I don't like to discourage you when you 'notice' things, but I didn't know how to respond. 'Sad' doesn't cover half of how I feel. Sad's like how you'd feel if your favourite teddy was chewed by the dog; or if the Christmas tree fell down and you had to pick up all the cracked glass baubles. But that's not me.

Anyway, I thought I'd write things down just in case you want to know later on. Or in case someone comes along who can share things with you and help you understand. And if you need anything, my love, go to Sally. Always remember that. She will always be there - even when I can't be.
Your loving Mum(my) xxxxxxx"

Through the window I could see Maggie wincing as she removed the lawn mower from her shed. It was heavy and cumbersome but its removal seemed some form of rite of passage. She would never need it again.

I handed the letter back to Dominic, and continued with the packing.

I was almost envious. The next of their life-adventures were just beginning.

Perhaps I should take inspiration and begin my own adventure.

Without Mark.

About the Author

Lesley Atherton was born in Scotland but has lived most of her life in Lancashire. She is settled with her small family and dog and enjoys the latter's company when writing.

In addition to this publication, she's also written 'Divine Intervention' (a story of twins, one good and one evil, and a universal narrator who tries to make a difference) and multiple short story collections under the title, 'Can't Sleep, Won't Sleep'.

If you enjoyed this book, you'll find more publications available from Scott Martin Productions on Amazon.

31912900R00038

Printed in Poland
by Amazon Fulfillment
Poland Sp. z o.o., Wrocław